That summer,
Frenchtown was a place
of Sahara afternoons,
shadows in doorways,
lingering evenings,
full of unanswered questions
and mysteries.

It was also the summer
of my twelfth birthday,
the summer
of Sister Angela
and Marielle LeMoyne
(even though she was dead)
and my brother, Raymond,
and all the others,
but especially my uncle Med
and my father.

And finally
it was the summer
of the airplane.

Other books
by Robert Cormier

Frenchtown Summer

ROBERT CORMIER

Published by
Dell Laurel-Leaf
an imprint of
Random House Children's Books
a division of Random House, Inc.
1540 Broadway
New York, New York 10036

Visit us on the Web! www.randomhouse.com/teens

Educators and librarians, for a variety of teaching tools, visit us at www.randomhouse.com/teachers

ISBN: 0-440-22854-9

RL: 7.4

Reprinted by arrangement with Delacorte Press

Printed in the United States of America

June 2001

10 9 8 7 6 5 4 3 2 1

OPM

To Bobbie, Peter, Chris and Renée
With Love, Dad

Frenchtown
Summer

1

Doorway Shadows

That summer in Frenchtown
in the days
when I knew my name
but did not know who I was,
we lived on the second floor
of the three-decker on Fourth Street.
From the piazza late in the afternoon
I watched for my father,
waiting for him to come home
from the Monument Comb Shop.
No matter how tired he was,

his step was quick.
He'd always look up, expecting to see me,
and that's why I was there,
not wanting to disappoint him
or myself.

That was the summer of my first paper route,
and I walked the tenement canyons
of Frenchtown
delivering *The Monument Times,*
dodging bullies and dogs,
wondering what I was doing
here on the planet Earth,
not knowing yet that the deep emptiness
inside me
was
loneliness.

I felt like a ghost
on Mechanic Street,
transparent as rain,
until the growling of Mr. Mellier's dog

restored my flesh and blood
and hurried me on my way.
I was always glad to arrive home,
where my mother,
who looked like a movie star,
welcomed me with a kiss and a hug.
My mother filled the tenement with smells,
cakes in the oven,
hot donuts in bubbling oil,
and hamburg laced with onions sizzling
in the black pan she called the Spider.
She loved books, lilac cologne,
and me.

My mother was vibrant,
a wind chime,
but my father was a silhouette,
as if obscured
by a light shining behind him.
He was closer to me waving from the street
than nearby in the tenement
or walking beside me.

On summer Saturdays,
the men gathered
at the Happy Times bar
or in Rouleau's Barber Shop
and talked about the Boston Red Sox
and the prospects of a layoff
at the Monument Comb Shop
while my brother, Raymond,
swapped baseball cards
in Pee Alley
with his best friend, Alyre Tournier.
I stood beside my father
as he listened
to what the men were saying,
smoking his Chesterfields,
and I wished I could be like him,
mysterious,
silent.

I was not famous in the schoolyard,
or on the street corners,
content to cheer for Raymond,

who was a star at everything,
baseball at Cartier's Field,
Buck Buck How Many Fingers Up?
in the schoolyard,
while I read
The Adventures of Tom Sawyer
or *A Study in Scarlet*
on the piazza,
avoiding the possibility
of dropping a fly ball in center field.

My paper route took me
from the green three-decker
next to the Boston & Maine railroad tracks
where downtown Monument
met Frenchtown,
along Mechanic
and all the numbered streets
from First to Twelfth.
My last customer was Mr. Lottier
at the end of Mechanic Street
next to the sewer beds.

I held my nose
as I tossed the paper to his piazza.
He always smiled
when he paid me on Friday,
as if his nose didn't work.

That summer,
Frenchtown was a place
of Sahara afternoons,
shadows in doorways,
lingering evenings,
full of unanswered questions
and mysteries.

It was also the summer
of my twelfth birthday,
the summer
of Sister Angela
and Marielle LeMoyne
(even though she was dead)
And my brother, Raymond,
and all the others,

but especially my uncle Med
and my father.

And finally
it was the summer
of the airplane.

2

The Haircut

How many times I have heard
the men at the Happy Times
talking about the famous dancer
in a London dressing room
who decided,
on a whim,
to cut off her tumbling locks
of auburn hair,
plunging Frenchtown
into a depression
a year later because
women all over the world

adopted her bobbed hairstyle
and did not require anymore
the fancy combs
and barrettes,
glittering with rhinestones,
dancing with sequins,
that paraded from the assembly lines
of the Frenchtown comb shops.
My father didn't work for a year.
Just a child then,
too young to understand
what was happening,
I only knew that my mother
did not smile anymore,
her voice like one long sad note
struck on a piano
when she read me stories,
while my father seemed to have gone away
even though I could see him clearly
in his kitchen chair by the window,
the silence in the tenement
a terrible noise
in my heart.

3

Red, Purple or Green

Moosock Brook
kept disappearing
as it flowed
through downtown Monument
and later Frenchtown,
red, purple or green,
depending on the dyes
dumped that day by the comb shops.
The brook slid
under Main Street
and reappeared

on Water Street,

colors hectic in the sunlight,

until it went unseen again

beneath the B&M railroad bridge,

before finally flowing

into the Meadows.

There it created

a sudden pool

into which Frenchtown kids,

Raymond among them,

plunged with glorious abandon,

emerging later,

dripping

red, purple or green

depending on the dyes

dumped that day

by the shops.

4

The Goggles

I wore my aviator helmet,
the goggles pushed up
on my head
in careless fashion,
striding through the streets
like a World War hero
home after aerial battles
over the trenches in France
until Hector Henault
tore the helmet from my head,
dashed it to the ground

and crushed the goggles
under his boots,
the sound
like my own bones cracking.
He paused to view his damage.
Holding the ruined goggles
in hands that trembled,
I withheld tears
as I screamed at him:
"Die, you dirty rat, die,"
(but silently, of course)
like James Cagney
in the movies.

Three days later,
Hector Henault was crushed
like my goggles
under the wheels of a Mack truck
on Mechanic Street
near Fifth.
They said he died instantly.
I was awestruck
by my power to kill.

On the fourth of July,
Oliver Randeau,
giggling,
lobbed a firecracker my way.
It exploded like a grenade
against my ear,
stunning my skull with pain.
Knowing the power I possessed,
I ignored the mad doorbells
ringing in my head
and looked at him.
Because he was stupid,
still in the sixth grade
at the age of fourteen,
with a left eye that often
went askew,
I decided
not to kill him.

Whenever I met him later,
on the sidewalks or in the empty lots,
I deflected his baleful stare
with a pitying smile.

Frowning, he always looked away.
Did he somehow know
that I held the power
of life and death over him?

I wondered whether
I should confess
this power of mine
to Father Balthazar
but instead vowed
never to use it again
even if absolutely
necessary.

5

My Father at Night

My father
often sat in the shadows
in the middle of the night,
The Monument Times
collapsed in his lap,
the dial on the Emerson radio
an orange moon in the dark,
the volume turned down.
As I crept by on my way
to the bathroom,
having been awakened

by a dream or a noise,
he looked up,
squinting,
then took his eyes away
from me.
I tried to speak, but no words came,
my voice drugged with sleep,
and he continued to stare
at nothing
while I glided like a ghost
to the bedroom,
my bathroom urge
forgotten.

Back in bed,
smelling the drifting smoke
of my father's cigarette,
I thought of him sitting up
like a sentry in the night,
guarding his family.

Yes but
why had he looked at me

as if I were a stranger
unknown to him,
in the kitchen
of the tenement
that was home?

I pretended
that my tears
were drops of sweat
because
the night was hot.

6

Riding the Rails

The Boston & Maine freight yards
drew Raymond and Paul Roget and me
across the iron bands of the tracks
to the boxcars.
We'd climb up,
then race along the roofs,
leaping from car to car
in breathtaking swoops,
pretending railroad bulls
(that's what they called them
in the movies at the Plymouth)

19

were chasing us,
blowing their whistles
and waving their billy clubs.
We'd take refuge in an empty car,
inhaling the aroma of faraway places
. . . Chicago . . . Omaha . . . Santa Fe . . .
dangling our feet at the door
like hoboes
riding the rails.

Our parents always reminded us
of Harold Donay,
who ran away from home
to ride the rails
and, one rainy night,
outside of Denver, Colorado,
slipped and fell
between the boxcars
and was sliced in half
by the wheels.

He was shipped home
in two parts,

people said,
and old Mr. Cardeaux,
the undertaker,
stitched him back together again
for the wake and funeral.

But we still stole across the tracks
and climbed the boxcars,
and outran the bulls . . .
although for a long time
I left the tenement
whenever my mother
picked up her needle and thread
to do her sewing.

7

My Irish Mother

My mother was Irish,
from a small town in Vermont,
her eyes the color of bruises,
her hair black
as the velvet on which
diamonds were displayed
in the windows of Brunelle's Jewelry Store.
Delicate as lace,
she was not like my sturdy aunts,
who stomped off to the comb shops
in the mornings,

or the vigorous aunts,
who stayed home with the babies,
scrubbing, ironing,
pummeling carpets on clotheslines.
Their hands swooped like trapezes
as they talked,
to help my mother understand
their Canuck words,
while my mother's hands
performed ballets.
Somehow they came to understand
each other
in a haphazard litany of language.

From magazines,
my mother scissored scenes
of country lanes,
farmhouses with smoke corkscrewing
from chimneys,
while her kitchen window
framed three-deckers,
streetlights and sidewalks,
and the comb shop roofs.

If her smile was sometimes wistful,
her laughter often ran silver
in the tenement.
She sighed at Raymond's roguish ways
as she caressed his cheek
and looked tenderly at me
in all my confusion.
Her eyes always lingered
on my father,
in what seemed to me
depths of love.

At those moments,
I looked at my father,
trying to read his eyes,
to find out
what was in his heart.
But he was as unknowable
as a foreign language.

8

The Third-Floor Piazza

In the massive heat
of a July afternoon,
delivering the *Times*
on Seventh Street,
I glanced up to see Mrs. Cartin
on her third-floor piazza,
hanging clothes on the line
that stretched like a limp rosary
from her three-decker
to the LeBlanc house next door.
Letting a blue shirt flutter

like a wounded bird
to the ground below,
she leaned forward,
her hands gripping the railing,
and rose as if on tiptoe,
lifting herself,
rising, rising,
higher and higher,
precariously poised,
like a bird before flight
—*but people can't fly*—
the throbbing in my throat
preventing me from calling:
"Don't jump, don't jump!"

She fell back from the railing,
like a balloon deflated.
As she turned away,
arms hugging her chest,
I saw tears on her cheeks
but told myself that
at that distance

they were tricks of summer sunlight
or my imagination.

That Sunday,
at the nine o'clock Mass,
she knelt in the third pew
alongside Mr. Cartin
and their two little girls.
She received Holy Communion,
eyes lowered
as she returned from the rail,
looking like a saint
in my prayer book.

I thought of how she had almost
followed that blue shirt
in its flight
to the yard below,
and placed the memory
in that dark place
where I kept all the secrets
of Frenchtown.

9

Forbidden Territory

Long ago,
before I was born,
the broken body
of Marielle LeMoyne
was found in the woods
at the bottom of Twelfth Street,
a wild place
of gnarled bushes
and stunted trees,
with a tortured path carving a shortcut
to the Acme Button Company

where Marielle worked
as a packer.
A yellow necktie
with black stripes
coiled like a snake
around her neck.

Children were warned
to stay away from those woods
but we often explored
that forbidden territory,
shivering with delicious fear,
trying to determine the exact spot
where she was murdered.
Her killer was never found
although a hobo was spied
leaping aboard a boxcar
headed west
the morning her body was discovered.
Marielle was buried
in St. Jude's Cemetery,
a marble angel
placed on her grave

by her father and mother,
who returned to Canada
the following summer
unable to withstand
the onslaught of memories
Frenchtown held for them.

Sometimes at night,
awaking suddenly,
hearing the chuffing of an engine
in the Boston & Maine freight yards,
I'd ponder the possibility
that the tramp had been
innocent after all,
remembering the rumors
that Marielle LeMoyne
had been three months pregnant
when she was slain.
Was it possible
that a murderer still stalked
the streets of Frenchtown,
kneeling in St. Jude's Church on Sundays,

buying hamburg steak
at Fournier's Meat Market,
drinking beer with the men,
my father among them,
at the Happy Times,
and, maybe,
maybe looking right into my eyes
as he passed me unidentified
on Third Street?

Or had he died?
Or simply moved away?

Those last thoughts
were like rosary beads of comfort
as I lay sleepless,
waiting for daylight
to arrive.

10

The Gaudy Ghosts

My uncles and aunts
came and went in my life
like gaudy ghosts,
playing bid whist at kitchen tables,
dancing the quadrille at weddings,
singing old songs on *le Jour de l'An*
at my pépère's house,
sitting on the evening piazzas,
the uncles gruff in their talk
and raucous with sudden laughter,
the women murmuring delights

of gossip,
gasping sometimes
at a surprising bit of news.
My uncle Philippe passed the collection basket
at the ten o'clock High Mass
Sundays at St. Jude's Church.
Uncle Albert was a clerk
at Fournier's Meat Market
and washed his hands all day long.
Raymond and I counted with delight
his many trips to the kitchen sink
as he listened to the Red Sox games
with my father,
the hanging towel near the sink
limp and damp
at the end of the afternoon.
My poor aunt Olivine
visited St. Jude's Church
every afternoon at four o'clock,
lighting a candle
for the soul of her child, Theo,
who spent only twelve minutes
in this world.

Years after he died,
she still dampened handkerchiefs
with her tears
and they waved
like small flags of distress
on her clothesline,
nobody able to come
to her rescue.
My uncle Eldore,
who laughed at everything,
claimed that her tears
came from a "sinus condition"
but we all still mourned
for poor Aunt Olivine.

The children in the family,
Raymond and me
and all my cousins,
made birthday visits
to my aunts and uncles,
passing our hats
like church collection baskets,
receiving nickels and dimes,

always a quarter from Uncle Med
and three shiny pennies
from Aunt Julienne,
who never married
and sewed and mended
for Frenchtown women
in Pépère's sitting room.

My uncles patted me on the head
as they walked by,
my aunts bestowed wet kisses
on my cheeks.
They called me Eugene
but most of them seldom
looked into my eyes
and I wondered
if they really knew
who I was.

11

White Shirts

My uncle Med
wore a white shirt
every day of the week,
buttoned to the top
for Sunday Mass, weddings and funerals,
but top button open
at the Monument Comb Shop,
where he wrestled boxes
in the shipping department.
He never wore a tie.

I picked up his shirts
every Saturday morning
at Henry Wong's Chinese Laundry
and laid them out neatly,
white as Communion wafers,
in his bureau drawer.
Friday night was my uncle's
downtown gambling night
and whether he won or lost,
he tossed me a quarter
the next day,
which paid my fare
to the Saturday movie at the Plymouth
with change left over
for a Baby Ruth or Mr. Goodbar
at Laurier's Drug Store.
He was my bachelor uncle,
target of my busy aunts,
who suggested,
sometimes arranged,
dates with available
but respectable Frenchtown girls

until he said:
"No more."
My aunts murmured
about a lost, unknown love
he still mourned
but raised their stubby fingers
to their lips
when he looked their way.

He lived in a two-room tenement
above LaGrande's Ice Cream Parlor,
the smell of chocolate
rising through the floorboards.
He never owned a car
but walked everywhere
to church and work,
tramped the woods and fields
of Frenchtown and Monument,
hiked occasionally
to Mount Wachusum,
a knapsack on his back,
blotches of sweat

on his white shirt.
Sometimes he invited
Raymond and me to join him.
He pointed out flowers and birds,
giving them names—
Queen Anne's lace by the side of the road,
barn swallows in sudden flight.
We always stopped
for sweet cider at Fontaine's Farm
on Ransom Hill
or banana splits
at the Boston Confectionery Store
downtown.

He was my happy uncle.
Yet sometimes I caught him
looking out the window,
so far away in his staring
that he'd forgotten I was there,
his shirts in my hands,
waiting for permission
to place them in his bureau.

What did he see outside his window
that I knew I would not see
even if I looked?

In my heart
was the knowledge,
lodged like a chunk of ice,
that I would never find out.

12

The Edges

The tombstones of St. Jude's Cemetery
at the far end of Mechanic Street
shimmered in the afternoon heat
as Raymond and I arrived,
a pilgrimage we made
when there was nothing else to do.
An ancient elm,
the cemetery's solitary tree,
guarded the entrance,
its benevolent shade
falling on the seven sad stones

that marked the graves
of the St. Jude nuns who died
far from the France of their birth.
We always stopped first
at the small stone
bearing the name of my cousin Theo,
who had lived only twelve minutes
twenty years before.
Marielle LeMoyne's marble angel
made us pause and look around
as if we were being watched
by whoever scrubbed her angel
free of bird droppings,
neatly combed the grass
and placed geraniums there
for Memorial Day.
As usual, we hurried past
the gray mausoleum
of the Menier family,
still not brave enough
to peek in the stained-glass windows
to see if the coffins
were visible.

We always ended our visits
at the Edges,
that unconsecrated ground
at the far end,
with the lonesome graves
of those who did not die
in the state of grace,
had taken their own lives
or abandoned their faith
or disgraced themselves
in ways I could only imagine.
No tombstones here,
only small tilted markers,
names long ago faded,
or no markers at all,
only lumps of earth
often decorated with debris.
We looked in vain
for the grave of Joe Latour,
who years ago had hanged himself
in a cell at the Monument police station
after his arrest
for drunken behavior

one Sunday morning
in front of St. Jude's Church.
He used to wander
the streets of Frenchtown,
weeping sometimes,
sleeping in Pee Alley,
which, Uncle Med claimed,
he baptized
on many occasions.

We were always glad
to leave the cemetery,
not looking behind us,
and I wondered
why we went there
in the first place.

13

A Sliver of Ice

Like setting a clock,
my mother adjusted
the octagonal card in the window,
telling Mr. Harrold, the ice man,
when he arrived on the street
how many pounds we needed—
fifty, seventy-five, one hundred.
Mr. Harrold wore a rubber apron
on his back
onto which he swung the blocks of ice
with huge tongs.

He lumbered up the stairs
without even grunting,
beads of sweat
like chips of ice
on his cheeks,
dumped the block into
the icebox in the kitchen.
My mother always offered him
a glass of Kool-Aid,
lime or orange.

Raymond, Alyre and I
waited for him to return
and when he arrived
he wielded the same pick
to shave wedges of ice
from the mounted blocks,
and handed them to us.
The ice, stingingly cold,
burned my lips and fingers
but at the same time
brought delicious
tingling to my tongue.

As Mr. Harrold went on his way
I stood with the other kids
in the pungent fragrance
of horse dung
and knew bliss
in a sliver
of ice.

14

"The Eyes Have It"

I emerged from Dr. Sampson's office,
("The Eyes Have It")
blinking into the sunlight,
and suddenly everything
had sharp edges,
the corners of buildings,
the curbstones,
a leaf tumbling
from the maple in Monument Park.
The glasses,
with steel frames,

were a strange weight on my nose.
A world suddenly vivid,
people's faces across the street
no longer blurs.
I saw the red spiderwebs
in the cheeks
of the cop directing traffic,
looked up to see
white clouds
clearly outlined
as if pasted on a page
in a child's coloring book.
And looked down to see
cracks of lightning
frozen in the sidewalk,
a shard of green glass
from a broken bottle
gleaming like a distant planet
fallen into the gutter.

Reeling as if drunk
on Uncle Philippe's home-brewed beer,
I knelt down to watch

a glistening ant
at the curb's rim,
and in my glorious generosity,
my state of grace,
did not squash it underfoot,
the world too sweet
and brightly lit
for anything,
even an ant,
to die today.

The glasses were a miracle,
bringing the sweet
gift of sight
until
in front of Laurier's Drug Store,
Ernie Forcier
placed his hands on his hips
and yelled to me
across the street:

"Hey, Four-Eyes."

15

Sister Angela

Love came to Frenchtown
in the middle of June
when Sister Angela arrived
on the last day of school
to teach piano
at the convent.
Meeting her one hazy afternoon
as I took a shortcut
through the convent gardens,
I fell into the violet pools
that were her eyes

and signed up for summer lessons,
soon plunging
into agonies of longing.
Dumb with desire,
I stumbled through my days and evenings
just as my fingers stumbled
as I struggled to play
"The Song of the Rose."
Delirious with her closeness
beside me on the bench,
the scent
of strong soap her perfume.
Her long fingers
were so lovely in their paleness
I longed to crush them
to my mouth
and kiss the palms of her hands,
not daring to dream
of touching her lips
with mine.
Mute in her presence,
tripping on the carpet's edge,
I was a pathetic lover.

By the time I had learned
to play "The Song of the Rose"
without tripping fingers
she had vanished,
gone to some unknown convent,
her sudden departure,
like her arrival,
unexplained,
a mystery,
just as so much of life
behind the shuttered windows
of the convent
was a mystery.

My anguish tore
my life into shreds
and I never played
the piano
again.

16

My Father's Pilgrimage

"So you're going."
My mother's voice
an off-key violin string,
while my father,
not answering,
tightened the knot
in his Sunday tie,
blue with cardinals flying
on the silk.

His white shirt glistened
in the bedroom mirror.
I watched him toss her question away
with the tilting of his chin.
He often didn't answer my mother
but his silences
could contain lightning,
at other times,
tenderness.
He shrugged into his Best Suit,
dark blue with faint stripes,
his suit for weddings and funerals
or special times
like the day he watched
President Franklin D. Roosevelt
waving from the final car
as the train slowed down
but did not stop
at the Monument depot.
"Spiffy," my mother always said
when my father put on his Best Suit.

But today, she said only:
"Go then."
Her voice
a violin string
snapping.

I followed him like a spy
through the thrumming Saturday crowds
on Third Street,
women clutching grocery bags,
the men lounging outside the Happy Times,
basking in the cellar smell of whiskey.
Mechanic Street led us downtown
while I dodged
from doorway to telephone pole
behind him.
He never turned around,
head down,
as if the sidewalk held a map
charting his way.
Through Monument Park
past the wartime statues,
and the Civil War cannon

aimed at the five-and-ten
across the street.
The North Side lay ahead,
big white houses
with wide verandas
and birdbaths on carpet lawns.
My father's steps faltered
and he stopped at a telephone pole.
Would he turn back?
He lit a Chesterfield,
then began to walk again,
more briskly now
as we passed Merryweather Lane
and Holly and Cranberry Avenues.
Frenchtown had streets,
not lanes or avenues,
piazzas, not verandas.
My father finally paused
at the two marble columns
guarding the entrance
to the Estate,
the home of Lanyard C. Royce,
owner of the Monument Comb Shop.

"Benefactor and Philanthropist,"
according to the *Times,*
reporting his death that week at age eighty-nine
in big black headlines on the front page.
"Inventor of machines that produced combs
eight hours a day without stopping."
I had seen his signature
scrawled on my father's Friday paychecks.
The *Times* did not report
what the men called Lanyard C. Royce
at the Happy Times:
Skinflint.
Strikebreaker.
A hard man, my father said at home,
striking a kitchen match
on the sole of his shoe.
I watched him enter the Estate,
diminishing in size
as he walked up the half-moon driveway,
past men gathered
near black limousines,
puffing at long cigars,

and he disappeared
into veils of smoke.

Waiting, I thought of the times
he dressed in that Best Suit
to visit Cardeaux's Funeral Home.
"Have to pay my respects," he'd say
and my mother never said,
"So you're going."
I lurked on the sidewalk,
keeping out of sight,
which was easy to do,
because the men with cigars
took no notice
of my presence
or my existence.

At home, after my mother
hung his Best Suit in the closet,
having enclosed it first
in cellophane,
they sat in the kitchen,

my father in his rocking chair,
my mother at the kitchen table,
smoothing invisible wrinkles
from the blue tablecloth.
I stared at the pages
of *Tom Sawyer*.
My mother looked at my father
and my father picked up the *Times*,
shook it as if to drop
the words on the floor
and began to read.
Or maybe pretended to read
like me.
My mother's pinched fingers made small tents
on the tablecloth.
The newspaper rustled
as my father turned the pages.

"Work is sacred," he declared
like a priest in the pulpit.

My mother continued
to make tents

and my father squinted at the newsprint

while I sat there

wondering

if I would ever solve

the mystery of my father.

17

The Dark Dance

"Arthur Colraine
has Saint Vitus' dance,"
Alyre Tournier announced.
I pictured Arthur
dancing madly, as a Gypsy violinist
blazed the air with music
near a campfire
like in the movies.
"Saint Vitus' dance
is a sickness,"

Alyre explained,
indignant with his information.

In Arthur's kitchen,
I watched his mother
feeding a blue shirt
into the wringer of the washing machine,
her wrist bruised purple
from the times
she'd caught her arm in the wringer.
All Frenchtown women
wore those purple badges.
Tilting her head, she said,
"He's awake now,"
as if a secret sound
had reached her ears.
Entering the shadowed bedroom,
I saw Arthur's sunken face
as if painted on a piece of cloth,
his hands moving in the air,
wild birds flying,
his fluttering fingers

plucking at unseen harp strings.
If his hands were birds in flight,
his eyes were birds
trapped in cages,
swinging this way and that,
unable to escape,
not looking at me,
or anything else in this world.
He was no longer Arthur Colraine,
climber of trees like Tarzan,
amazing at arithmetic
in Sister Gertrude's classroom,
but a depraved stranger,
nameless,
an apparition,
and I fled the bedroom,
did not remember later
whether I said "Thank you"
to his mother.
Running down Fifth Street,
conscious of my hands,
I stopped in terror
—were they fluttering?—

had I somehow caught
that terrible affliction?

Pronounced cured at last,
Arthur Colraine
forever after
walked among us
alone and apart,
in the schoolyard,
on the sidewalks,
and one of my sins
is that I never
spoke to him
again.

18

The Confessional

In the confessional
at St. Jude's Church,
I knelt in turmoil,
only a shimmering curtain
protecting me
from the ears of my classmates
six feet away in the pews
while Father Balthazar,
ear pressed to the small screen,
urged me to
"Speak up, speak up."

I recited my thin catalog
of sins:
talking during Mass,
swearing ten times,
disobeying my parents,
losing my temper,
routine disclosures
of sins that I wasn't even sure
I had committed,
but I had to confess
something.
Then the long pause,
hearing the rustling
of my classmates,
wondering if they had heard my whispers
as I had sometimes heard theirs.
Father Balthazar waited,
as if listening
for the sin
I could not find the courage
to confess.
"That's all," I finally said,
wondering if priests could see

the stains on our souls.
I heard my penance:
"Recite ten Our Fathers
and ten Hail Marys
and promise to do better,"
his voice scratching at the screen.

Limp with relief
but hounded
by that unspoken sin
—those moist moments
in my bed at night—
I wondered whether
the sin of touching
and the sin of silence
obliterated my state of grace,
dooming me forever
to the fires of Hell
as I swallowed the white Host
that was the body of Jesus Christ
Sunday
after Sunday.

19

The Birthday

We never called them
birthday parties
but my mother always invited friends
for cake and ice cream,
the cake,
my favorite,
golden,
with butter frosting,
ice cream a dripping rainbow
of vanilla, chocolate and strawberry,
and candles to blow out,

my gift a flashlight,
silver
like a Buck Rogers ray gun.
I was dazzled by the light
it splashed
on walls and ceilings
and ran to the bedroom,
sending its radiance under the bed,
lighting up
the small gray ghosts of dust.

That night in bed,
Raymond snoring softly,
my father nodding in his chair,
a Chesterfield burning down
in the ashtray,
I flashed the light
endlessly around the room
like a prison searchlight
or a beacon guiding ships
on stormy seas,
and fell asleep

like a lightbulb
going dark.

In the morning,
awaking before Raymond,
I sleepily tested
my newest treasure,
but no beam came forth,
the flashlight dead.
Not knowing that batteries
could be replaced,
I huddled in the sheet,
ashamed of my night's flagrancy
and realized
that nothing lasts
forever.

20

Jackstones

On a Saturday walk with Uncle Med
a sudden downpour
sent us scurrying for refuge
to St. Jude's Cemetery's old elm tree.
When the rain became mere dripping
as if the elm were weeping,
we waited for a rainbow
that never appeared.
Raymond asked if Uncle Med
knew where Joe Latour was buried.

Over the damp gravel
he led us to the Edges,
and to a pathetic mound of earth,
a broken whiskey bottle,
not a stone, marking its spot.
Uncle Med said:
"Poor Joe, a nice guy.
We went to school together,
but he quit in the fourth grade."
It amazed me that my uncle
had known a man who'd hanged himself.
Going past Marielle LeMoyne's grave,
Raymond asked:
"Did you know her, too?"
Resting his hand
on the head of the marble angel,
Uncle Med said:
"We all grew up together,
your father, too.
Marielle was a good girl,
wild sometimes,
could dance all night,

wore too much makeup,
but sweet,
a sweet young girl."

That night,
I dreamed of Marielle LeMoyne
playing jackstones,
a young girl suddenly,
her skirt spread around her legs
as she sat on the sidewalk,
bouncing the small red ball
and grabbing a silver jackstone
with long pale fingers.
Uncle Med and my father
and someone I knew was Joe Latour
watched her play,
and they, too, were young
like Marielle.
One of them,
I could not tell which,
his face shadowed,
snatched the jackstone
from Marielle's fingers.

She began to cry,
tears dissolving her face,
her black flowing hair
suddenly turned red,
red like blood,
was blood,
flowing over her body,
as the boys,
shadows now,
ran away
with all her jackstones.
And I woke up.

In the night's stillness,
the B&M trains silent,
my thudding heart the only sound,
I vowed never to return
to St. Jude's Cemetery,
another vow
I did not keep.

21

The Balloon Man

Everyone made fun
of Omer LaFerge,
who stood like a balloon
at the corner of Fifth and Mechanic,
clicking his false teeth,
while kids gathered around him
as if he were a sideshow attraction
at the Captain Clyde Circus,
which came to Frenchtown every three years.
Kids poked at his stomach
or pinched his cherub cheeks

while Omer swayed back and forth
as if his shoes were made of lead.
He was offered hard candy
so that we could hear his false teeth
clicking
as he tried to chew,
spittle on his lips,
a smile on his face,
eager to please everyone,
ageless as a statue
waiting to be
defaced.

Then one day
he simply wasn't there
anymore.

22

Doorway Flowers

I always hurried
by the house
where a bouquet of flowers
hung beside the front door
announcing that someone had died,
and a coffin
in the parlor
awaited the arrival of people
who would kneel,
murmuring prayers
in the suffocating scent

of other flowers.
The doorway flowers
were always white,
cupped in white baskets.
Even when they were removed
after the funeral,
I still hurried by that house,
my eyes averted.

One Easter morning
my father presented my mother
with a bouquet of white flowers,
which she placed on
the mahogany end table
in the parlor,
and whenever I walked by
I held my breath
so that I wouldn't inhale
the smell of death.

23

The Bald Spot

On *le Jour de l'An,*
that first day of the new year,
Pépère's sons and daughters
visited him in the morning
after Mass,
knelt before him
for his blessing,
the father and children repeating
the ancient ritual brought
from the old life

on the banks of the Richelieu River
in the Province of Québec.

I watched one winter morning
my father kneeling,
head bowed,
at his father's knees,
saw for the first time
the small oval of whiteness
at the back of his head.
In a burst of knowledge,
I saw that he was not ageless,
after all,
and would die someday.

Now, in August heat,
in the pantry,
as my father bent down
to remove
the brimming tray at the bottom of the icebox,
I saw that spot of baldness,
whiter, wider now,

his hair thinner,
revealing his pale scalp,
and I fled the tenement,
clattered down the stairs,
in sudden rushing panic
running to—
where?—
I was blinded
by the knowledge
that there was
no safe place
to run to.

24

Summer Sunday

Once every summer
the family spent a Sunday
at Moccasin Pond.
I sat squeezed between
my cousins Francine and Ernie
in my uncle Eldore's Chevy,
baskets on the floor
bulging with baloney sandwiches,
quart bottles of orange Kool-Aid
clinking in paper bags.

On the burning sands,
I hovered in my bathing suit,
straps biting my frail shoulders,
while my cousins frolicked,
splashing and diving,
pushing and shoving,
delighting in the freedom
from Frenchtown pavement.

I held back,
knowing that the instant
I removed my glasses
the world would blur,
the pond become a monster
lapping at my feet,
while my cousin Freddie called:
"Hey, Eugene, come on in,
the water's wet."

I spent
the rest of the day
waiting
to go home.

25

My Silent Uncle

My uncle Jules
limped through the streets of Frenchtown,
his right leg not synchronized
with the rest of his body,
walking as if trying to maintain
his balance
on a tilting sidewalk.
He was my silent uncle,
sat in the back pew at Sunday Mass,
converted the shed at Pépère's house
into a bedroom,

did not join the family
at the supper table
but took his plate
back to his room
to eat by himself.
He had been hurt
when prayers brought
three hundred pounds
of combs and brushes
down on him as he walked by,
the sound of his legs breaking
like gunshots
in the shipping department.

(My uncle Med told me all this
as we hiked up Ransom Hill
toward Pepper Point.)

Uncle Jules was seventeen years old,
waiting to be drafted any moment
and sent overseas
to die in the trenches in France
when the crates fell,

saving him from war.
That's what my pépère believed
and why he had spent hours
in St. Jude's Church
kneeling in prayer,
lighting candles,
rising each morning
for the five o'clock nuns' Mass,
gulping Holy Communion
like a starving man.
At the end of nine days,
the length of a novena,
the crates fell
in an avalanche of boxes.

Every year
on *le Jour de l'An*
Pépère waited in vain
for Uncle Jules to kneel before him,
seeking his blessing.
As the morning turned to afternoon
tears spilled from Pépère's eyes
like blood from wounds.

26

The Frenchtown Beat

Everybody said
Officer O'Brien was a good cop.
His beat was Frenchtown
and he patrolled the streets
as if strolling in a park
but a deadly gun rode at his side
and a black billy club hung from his hip.
He kicked the behinds of kids
who misbehaved,
manhandled the drunks
who became unruly at the Happy Times

and sent them home to their wives.
His smile
was quick
but his black eyes could see
into your soul
and make it shrivel.
They said he had a scar on his shoulder
from a bullet fired
by a robber who'd held up
the Merchants' Bank downtown.
Despite the wound,
the good cop O'Brien
brought the robber down
with a tackle,
the sidewalk behind him
veined with his blood.
They also said he was in love
with Mrs. Rancoeur on Fifth Street,
whose husband often left town
for days at a time,
sometimes weeks,
and returned without explanation.
No one ever saw the good cop O'Brien

and Mrs. Rancoeur together.
He only tipped his hat to her
when she passed by on Third Street,
arms bundled with groceries,
her two children at her side.
"Rumors," my father said,
shaking his newspaper
while my mother looked dreamy,
staring out the window.
"They're such nice people," she said.
"Life is so sad sometimes."

While my father
kept reading the newspaper.

27

My Father at Work

Sometimes I brought my father's lunch
to the comb shop
and the foreman, Mr. Leonard,
allowed me to ascend the wooden stairs
to the second floor,
where my father worked
at the shaking machine,
which rained bristles down
into celluloid shells
that would later become hairbrushes.
The smell of celluloid,

sweet and acid at the same time,
lanced my eyeballs
and long before had penetrated
my father's pores
so that even after a bath
he carried the smell of the shop with him
like a disease
for which there was no cure.
He always frowned when he saw me there,
and kept on working
while I placed the brown bag
with his two sandwiches,
either baloney or spiced ham,
and a piece of fruit,
a pear maybe or an apple,
on the windowsill.
He never spoke
(I would not have heard him, anyway,
above the noise of the machines
that trembled the floor
beneath my feet)
but nodded his thanks

before his eyes showed me the way out.
Sometimes my father worked
at the bubbling vat,
which spilled hot globs of cement
onto the celluloid shells,
splashing on his hands,
blisters the size of dimes
like evil puddles on his flesh.
He never complained,
sat in his kitchen chair after work
sipping the cold beer
my mother served him
from the icebox,
his shoulders sagging,
a wan smile on his face
as she handed him the *Times*
before bustling off to the pantry
to prepare supper.
Somehow, the beer softened
the harsh angles of his cheekbones
and his eyelids often fluttered,
almost closing,

and he half-dozed in the smells
of hamburg frying,
or sometimes sausage,
nodding,
listening to her voice
the way he listened to music sometimes
on the radio,
a half-smile on his lips,
as if he enjoyed not only what she was saying
but also the sound of her voice.
I loved those moments
just before supper,
my father half-dozing in the chair
basking in my mother's voice,
and my mother
humming sometimes
as she peeled potatoes,
glancing at me once in a while
as if we shared a secret.

I didn't know what the secret was,
I only knew that we both loved

my father,
and I knew he loved my mother
by the way he looked at her
but I wondered if he loved
me, too.

28

The Disappearance

Suddenly,
my uncle Med
did not occupy his third-row pew
at St. Jude's nine o'clock Mass,
did not punch the time clock
at seven A.M. Monday at the comb shop,
did not join the other men
at the Happy Times after supper.
My father and Uncle Philippe
encountered only silence
when they knocked at the door

of his tenement
while I hung back near the stairway.
Mr. LeBlanc, the landlord,
let them in with his key.
The smell oozing into the hallway
was stronger than chocolate.
"Don't light a match,"
Mr. LeBlanc yelled.
"Go home,"
my father commanded me
over his shoulder.
The sound of windows being thrown open
followed me downstairs.

Later, from the pantry,
I heard the low voices
from Pépère's kitchen.
"No note!"
Whispers and murmurs.
Then Pépère's voice.
If lightning had a tongue
it would speak the way
Pépère spoke

at that moment.
"He will not be buried
in the Edges!"
My uncle Med was buried
beside young Cousin Theo
in what my father called
the family plot.
"Room for ten more,"
someone said.

I did not cry.
My eyes burned
but tears would not come
to melt the frozen wasteland
in my chest.

My mother and my aunts
went to Uncle Med's tenement
for his belongings.
I walked behind them,
silent as a shadow.
In Uncle Med's bedroom,
I took a small black box

down from the closet shelf
and opened it to a dazzle
of silver and gold,
a tangle of tie pins,
some plain, some fancy,
one shaped like a rifle,
the ruby on another
catching the afternoon sun.

But he never
wore a tie.

That night,
I dreamed about a black and yellow snake
coiling itself around
the old elm at St. Jude's Cemetery,
black tongue flickering
at my feet as I climbed,
slowly, slowly,
away from the darting tongue
while down below
Uncle Med watched,
unmoving,

his eyes as blank
as coins.

My screams woke up the tenement,
my father instantly beside me
on the bed,
and I cried at last
but did not know
for whom.

29

Mysteries

In the wasteland
of a dying August,
the last days of vacation,
as I delivered the *Times*
in sun-struck streets,
my thoughts went to the mysteries
of the summer,
wondering what had happened
to Omer LeFerge
and in what convent

Sister Angela now taught the piano.
On Seventh Street,
I looked up at the piazza
where Mrs. Cartin had stood
like a bird about to take flight.
Would she someday make that leap?
I remembered what my mother said:
"Life is sad sometimes."
I thought of the mysteries
in my own family
(Did Pépère's prayers
perform a dark miracle
for Uncle Jules?)
and the things I did not want
to think about,
like the sins I didn't tell
Father Balthazar
in the confessional,
but most of all,
most of all,
the spot in the backyard
where I had buried
Uncle Med's tie pins.

But
I
did
not
want
to
think
about
him.

So I delivered the newspapers,
the heat coming off the pavement
like steam from a kettle,
no dogs barking,
no cars passing,
piazzas shrouded
in afternoon shadows.

On Fifth Street,
heading home,
my heart as empty
as my newspaper bag,
I saw
the airplane.

The Airplane

First,
a wink of color,
orange,
in the corner of my eye,
at the far end of an alley
between two three-deckers.
I tossed my paper bag
to the sidewalk
and followed the flash of orange
to a backyard,
where I saw,

unbelievably,
an airplane.
Orange, yes,
with lightning streaks
of white
on the fuselage,
two wings,
a biplane,
the kind of airplane
aviators flew during the World War
over the trenches of France and Germany,
like the airplanes I read about
in magazines like *Wings* and *Aces*
at Laurier's Drug Store.
Aviator goggles dangled from the cockpit
as if left there a moment before
by the pilot.

An airplane in a Frenchtown backyard?
Impossible!
No room to land or take off
in the narrow backyards
behind the tall three-deckers.

Mesmerized,
I stood there for a moment,
then left in a frenzy,
running through the alley,
heard the gasps of my breathing
as I searched the streets
for someone to tell
of my discovery.

At home, Raymond
and Alyre Tournier
tossed a ball between them,
the black-taped ball
thudding into their gloveless palms.
"There's an airplane in a backyard
on Fifth Street,"
I announced.
They kept throwing the ball to each other.
"It's real—I saw it."
Watching the ball trace
a rainbow arc between them.
Desperate, I cried:
"It's really there.

An orange airplane."
My voice on the still summer air
echoed through the neighborhood
and a few kids emerged
from doorways and piazzas,
Leon Montaigne and Paul Roget
and Henri Latour,
among others.
"Come on and see," I urged.

"Okay, okay," Raymond said,
striding toward me with his athlete's walk,
swinging his shoulders.
He never got excited about anything
except home runs, double plays
and stretching a double into a three-bagger.

I led the caravan down Mechanic Street,
the focus of all eyes.
I had never hit a home run
but I had discovered an airplane
in a Frenchtown backyard.

We turned into Fifth Street
and they followed me through the alley
as I looked for the flash of orange
that suddenly wasn't there.
Arriving,
I saw only the abandoned garden,
and shriveled tomato plants.

And
no
airplane.

Raymond shook his head,
looking at me with the kind of contempt
—or was it pity?—
he bestowed on players
who struck out with the bases loaded.
Leon and Alyre and Henri straggled away,
glancing at me as they went.
Somebody laughed,
maybe Leon,
and somebody muttered words

I refused to interpret.
Later, I walked home alone
in disgrace.

That evening,
in the gentle twilight
of late summer,
the families gathered on the piazzas
and the small patches of lawn
and talked mildly and gossiped,
while Raymond and the others
played ball in the street.
The men's cigarettes
glowed like fireflies
in the gathering dusk
and the smell of home-brewed beer
spiced the air.

I sat alone on the steps,
the light too dim for reading,
glad to remain twilight-hidden,
although Alyre Tournier,

after catching a fly ball,
muttered, "An airplane,"
shaking his head
with false pity
as he walked away.
When darkness obscured
the flight of the ball,
the game broke up
and the players strayed
toward the piazzas
in lazy end-of-day strides.
A sudden stillness fell
as if fed
by an evening breeze.

My father flicked his cigarette butt
into the air.
We watched it spiral
like a small comet
to the sidewalk.
Looking off into the deepening dusk,
he said,
his voice clear as struck crystal:

"Funny thing.
I saw an airplane this morning
on the way to the shop,
in the backyard of three-deckers
on Fifth Street."

A match flared as he lit
another cigarette.
"But it was gone
when I looked again
on the way home."
Smoke circled his head
like a halo.

He motioned to me.
"Eugene saw it, too."

Raymond looked at me,
mouth agape with astonishment,
and Alyre frowned,
hitching his pants.
Kids approached,
as if coming out of hiding places.

In the descending night,
I told them again and again
about the orange airplane,
the goggles dangling
from the cockpit.

And the night was sweeter
than a cherry soda
at the Happy Times.

The next day,
I waited for my father as usual
late in the afternoon,
standing this time
at the banister of the piazza.
Seeing him at last,
I ran to greet him,
throwing my arms around him,
losing myself in the aroma
of celluloid and smoke
and burned kitchen matches.

I looked up at him.

He passed his hand across my head,
rumpling my hair,
and said:
"I know. I know."

And we walked home together
in the tender sunlight
of a Frenchtown summer.

The Best in Teen Fiction
from ROBERT CORMIER

THE CHOCOLATE WAR

BEYOND THE CHOCOLATE WAR

I AM THE CHEESE

**AFTER THE
FIRST DEATH**

**IN THE MIDDLE
OF THE NIGHT**

Look for the riveting new novel from
ROBERT CORMIER

A seven-year-old girl is brutally murdered.
A twelve-year-old boy named Jason was
the last person to see her alive—except,
of course, for the killer. Unless *Jason* is
the killer.

Coming soon from Delacorte Press

ISBN: 0-385-72962-6